A TEMPLAR BOOK

Produced by The Templar Company plc,
Pippbrook Mill, London Road, Dorking, Surrey, RH4 1JE,
Great Britain.

First published in USA in 1990 by GALLERY BOOKS, an imprint
of W.H. Smith Publishers, Inc., 112 Madison Avenue, New York,
New York 10016.
First published in Canada in 1990 by W.H. Smith Ltd,
113 Merton Street, Toronto, Canada M45 1A.
Gallery Books are available for bulk purchase for sales promotion
and premium use. For details write or telephone the Manager of
Special Sales. W.H. Smith Publishers, Inc., 112 Madison Avenue,
New York, New York 10016 (212) 532 – 6600.

Designed by Philip Hargraves
Color separations by J. Film Process, Bangkok, Thailand.
Printed and bound in Great Britain by MacLehose and Partners Ltd.

ISBN 0-8317-5649-7

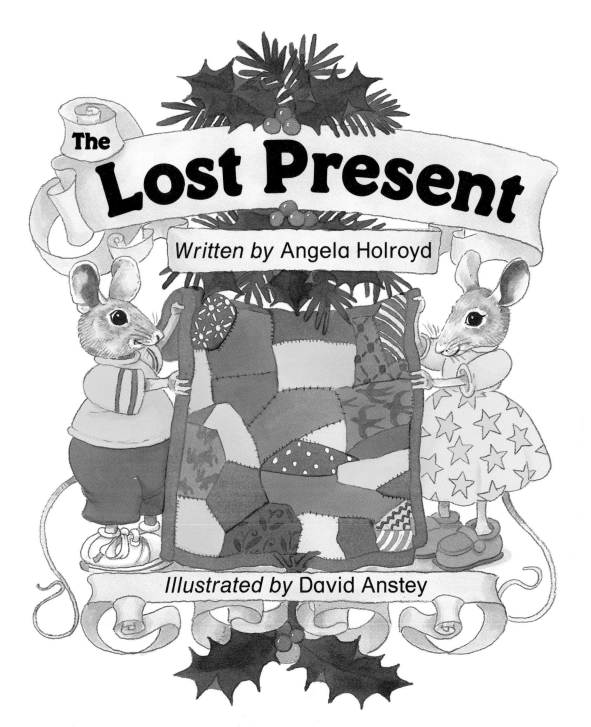

The Lost Present

Written by Angela Holroyd

Illustrated by David Anstey

GALLERY BOOKS
An Imprint of W. H. Smith Publishers Inc.
112 Madison Avenue
New York City 10016

Beneath the floor at number 5 Mill Road lived a family of mice. Their home was called the Mouse Hole. It was two days before Christmas and they were all very excited – all that is except Tommy. They had heard from Uncle Joseph in the country and he and Cousin Marmaduke were coming to stay for Christmas.

"I don't know why you are all so happy," moaned Tommy, as they all sat around the table. Mother Mouse was reading out the letter that had arrived that morning.

"It's fun to have family for Christmas," she beamed.

"Not when you have to share your room with a great big oaf," said Tommy. "MARMADUKE! What kind of a name is that?"

"Don't be so horrible," said Tilly, his sister. "Marmaduke is very kind."

"He is also *stupid*!" sneered Tommy. "Last time he came here he didn't even know what a street lamp was. He was scared! Imagine being scared of a light."

"He lives in the country," said Mother Mouse. "Everything is different in a city."

"Well, I don't care. I don't want him here." Tommy stamped out of the door.

"Oh dear!" said Mother Mouse. "I do hope they become friends. Go and talk to him Tilly. I have so much to do." And she bustled off to the larder to check her hazelnut puddings, cheese pies, and blackberry tarts.

Tilly found Tommy sulking in his bedroom.

"Why don't you like Cousin Marmaduke, Tommy?" she asked.

"Because he is a scaredy-cat. Why, even the footsteps of the people upstairs made him shiver and quiver."

"I think you're being very nasty. He had to get used to them, that's all. I bet you're scared of some things."

"I am not. I am not scared of anything!" he said, and he puffed out his chest.

"Good, I am glad you're not," said his sister, "because I need you to help me bring Mother's Christmas present *across the big hall*." She whispered the last bit.

The big hall was upstairs where the humans lived. Tilly had made her mother a quilt beneath the floor of the sewing room. All the needles, threads and materials were kept in a big basket. At night when everyone was asleep Tilly had slipped into the room and borrowed scraps that no one else could use, to make a quilt. Now it was finished. It would have to be taken to the Mouse Hole.

"I would like to move it tonight," she said. Tommy shook his head.

"You're not going to get me creeping around upstairs at night," he said. "What about the cat?"

"But I must get it," said Tilly. "I really want to give Mother a nice present this Christmas."

"I don't know why you are bothering. I'm only going to give her a card." said Tommy. Tilly could not believe her ears.

"You can't only give her that," she said. "That's not a good present."

"It is good enough for me," Tommy said. "I don't know why you are making all this fuss." Tilly felt sad. Poor Mother.

"Well I want to give her the quilt. I have made it specially for her. Please . . . please help me Tommy."

"Oh, all right." Tommy agreed just to keep Tilly quiet.

Later that night when all the humans were asleep, Tilly and Tommy crept out of the tiny hidden doorway behind the coat stand. They scurried across the shiny floor and under the sewing room door. Tilly found the quilt she had hidden under the floor. Quietly they started to carry it back, when Tommy heard a noise. He stopped and put his finger to his mouth.

"Shush!" he whispered. Tilly listened but all she could hear was a clock ticking somewhere. She shook her head and beckoned Tommy on. They took a few more steps when… Crea…eak!

"Ooo ah!" cried Tommy. What was that? They both pricked up their ears. Their whiskers stiffened. Before their eyes the kitchen door opened and a large striped creature walked out. The CAT!

Tommy let go of the quilt and fled. Tilly scampered as fast as she could, dragging the quilt. But it was no good. The cat was right behind her. She dropped the quilt and ran under the coat stand. The cat picked up the quilt in its teeth. Poor Tilly – she watched as the cat dropped the quilt down the back of the big chest of drawers at the side of the room.

"That will teach them!" thought the cat as he went back into the kitchen to drink a saucer of milk.

With two big tears rolling down her cheeks, Tilly scurried back to the Mouse Hole and into Tommy's room. He was pretending to be asleep so he didn't have to explain to his sister why he had run away. But Tilly knew he was awake – the bedcovers were shaking!

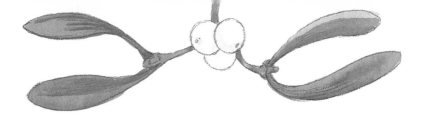

The next day was Christmas Eve. Everyone was busily decorating the Mouse Hole. Garlands and ornaments were hung over the doorways. Silver tinsel stars were hung from nails in the floorboard ceiling. It all looked very bright and cheery. But Tilly was still very upset. How could she get her mother's present from behind the chest of drawers? Tommy would not even talk about it. All he said was, "I was stupid enough to go with you last night. You're not going to get me to go *again* – that cat is very dangerous!"

Later that afternoon Uncle Joseph and Cousin Marmaduke arrived. Cousin Marmaduke was wearing his country clothes – a warm woolen jacket and enormous boots.

"Just look at him!" Tommy laughed.

"Shush!" said Tilly. "You will hurt his feelings."

"Teatime everybody!" called Mother Mouse. "Come and sit down." It was a delicious tea. Cheese pastries, blackberry tart, rosehip jelly, and raspberry juice. Mrs Mouse had been storing food since the summer.

"That was scrummy," said Marmaduke. "Thank you."

Mrs Mouse blushed with pride. Tommy only giggled.

"Scrummy! What a stupid word," he snickered to himself.

"Why don't you take Cousin Marmaduke for a walk?" said Father Mouse crossly.

"I can't," said the naughty Tommy. "I've got something important to do," and he rushed out of the room.

Poor Mrs Mouse. She was so ashamed of her son.

"I'll take you into the garden, if you like," said Tilly. The pair scampered off, leaving the grown-up mice behind.

Sitting under a hawthorn bush Tilly told Cousin Marmaduke about the lost Christmas present.

"I so wanted to give mother a beautiful present this year," said Tilly. "Christmas is such a special time. It's a time when you can say thank you to someone for all the good things they have done for you. I won't feel right if I haven't got a special present."

Cousin Marmaduke nodded. He had brought presents for everyone, including his cousin Tommy!

"I could try to get it for you," said Cousin Marmaduke shyly.

"But what about the cat?" asked Tilly. "He will smell us."

"Not if we fill our pockets with lavender."

"Mother has some lavender," cried Tilly. "Oh! . . . you are clever." Marmaduke's face turned red.

Later that night the pair sneaked out of the door behind the coat stand. Each of their pockets was filled with lavender. Marmaduke carried a small blue bag. As quietly as they could they scurried across the hall. Silently they tried to climb the chest of drawers, but it was so highly polished they kept slipping.

"I thought this might come in useful," said Cousin Marmaduke. Out of his blue bag he took a piece of rope and made a loop at one end. He swung it around in the air then up . . . up . . . UP. The loop landed around a carved piece of wood at the very top of the chest. Cousin Marmaduke held the bottom of the rope for Tilly to climb. When it came to his turn, Tilly was surprised at how quickly he managed to scramble up.

Once at the top, Cousin Marmaduke took three sticks out of his bag and fitted them together. He had made up the fishing rod he'd borrowed from Tommy.

He dropped the hook and line behind the chest of drawers and started fishing . . .

"I've got something! I've got something!" he cried excitedly a few minutes later. He pulled and pulled. The rod bent. "It's heavy," he panted. "Here it is . . . Oh!" On the end of his hook was someone's scarf.

Just then the kitchen door creaked. Both mice hid in the shadows. They kept very, very still. Out of the kitchen came the cat. His large yellow eyes glowed in the dark. He stretched and yawned. Tilly and Cousin Marmaduke saw his long white fangs and their fur stood on end. The cat twitched his whiskers. He was sure he had heard squeaks. Where had they come from? He turned his head and twitched his nose. He seemed to be looking straight at them. What was that strong smell? It did not smell of mice. Tilly and Cousin Marmaduke held on to each other in fright. The cat walked up and down the hall slowly. Then he sat at the foot of the chest of drawers and slowly licked one paw!

Tilly and Cousin Marmaduke held their breath. The cat seemed to stay there for ages. Tilly was beginning to feel that she could stay still no longer when the cat stretched and padded quietly back into the kitchen. The lavender had worked!

Cousin Marmaduke let out a long breath – phew! Then he lowered his fishing line again. It hooked on to something else. Slowly he lifted the rod up. Yes, there is was, Tilly's quilt. Very, very quietly the pair scrambled down the rope, holding the quilt in their teeth. Before they knew it, they were safely back in the Mouse Hole. Tilly rushed into Tommy's room. She shook him awake.

"Look! Look! Cousin Marmaduke is so clever. He has gotten the quilt back."

Tommy slowly opened his eyes. He looked at Tilly and Cousin
Marmaduke . . . and turned over. "So what?" was all he said. Tilly
pointed to the bed that her mother had made up for Marmaduke.

"Forget him," she whispered. "Go to bed. I will see you in the
morning . . . and thank you. Thank you very much."

25

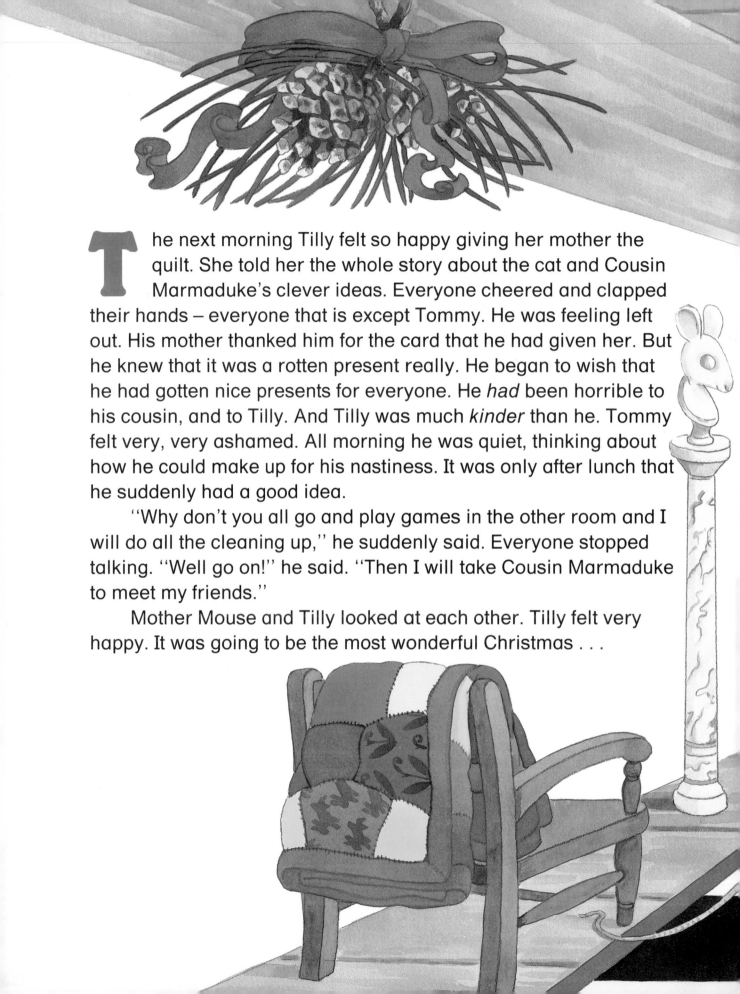

The next morning Tilly felt so happy giving her mother the quilt. She told her the whole story about the cat and Cousin Marmaduke's clever ideas. Everyone cheered and clapped their hands – everyone that is except Tommy. He was feeling left out. His mother thanked him for the card that he had given her. But he knew that it was a rotten present really. He began to wish that he had gotten nice presents for everyone. He *had* been horrible to his cousin, and to Tilly. And Tilly was much *kinder* than he. Tommy felt very, very ashamed. All morning he was quiet, thinking about how he could make up for his nastiness. It was only after lunch that he suddenly had a good idea.

"Why don't you all go and play games in the other room and I will do all the cleaning up," he suddenly said. Everyone stopped talking. "Well go on!" he said. "Then I will take Cousin Marmaduke to meet my friends."

Mother Mouse and Tilly looked at each other. Tilly felt very happy. It was going to be the most wonderful Christmas . . .